A Job for Donald and Douglas
Reading Book

Illustrated by Niall Harding
Written by Brenda Apsley

Thomas the Tank Engine & Friends

A BRITT ALLCROFT COMPANY PRODUCTION

Based on The Railway Series by The Rev W Awdry

© Gullane (Thomas) LLC 2003

Published in Great Britain in 2003 by Egmont Books Limited, 239 Kensington High Street, London, W8 6SA
Printed in China   ISBN 0 7498 5767 6

1 3 5 7 9 10 8 6 4 2

This pre-reading programme ...

is designed to encourage an early confidence in reading.

It features the 45 frequent-use words as set out in the

National Curriculum, plus key vocabulary from the

Thomas Learning programme.

Listening to stories provides a very strong motivation for children to make the effort

to learn to read themselves. Thomas and friends are well-loved characters.

Children need exciting characters in stories so they will enjoy learning to read.

There is lots of repetition of key words and phrases. This encourages recognition of

words and the link between their sounds and shapes. Your child will also begin to

predict what is coming next, thus connecting written and spoken words, enabling

them to 'read'.

To get the most out of the Look and Say books:

· read the stories several times with your child on different occasions;

· read the speech in a lively, animated style and point to the words;

· encourage your child to read aloud the words he/she has learned.

Other activities to enjoy

· **Follow the train tracks**

   Children will trace with their finger from left to right in preparation for reading and writing.

· **Find the pictures**

   Children will learn to observe small details in this activity.

· **Spot the difference**

   Children will compare two pictures - a skill used in reading when distinguishing letter shapes and words.

Donald and Douglas were twin engines.

4

One day, The Fat Controller came to
see them.

"I want one of you to go to the Yard,"
he said.

"I will go!" said Donald.
"Please send me."

"No, I will go," said Douglas.
"Send me."

"I can go faster," said Donald.
"Send me."

"No, I can go faster," said Douglas.

"Please send me!" said Donald and Douglas.

"Me! Me!" they said.
"Send me!"

"Please be quiet!"
said The Fat Controller.

"Who will I send?" he said to Thomas.

"I know who to send," said Thomas.

"Is it me? Is it me?" said Donald and Douglas.

"No, it is not you," said Thomas.
"It is me!"

"I am fast. I am quick.
Send me to the Yard!"

"I will!" said The Fat Controller.
"Off you go, Thomas!"

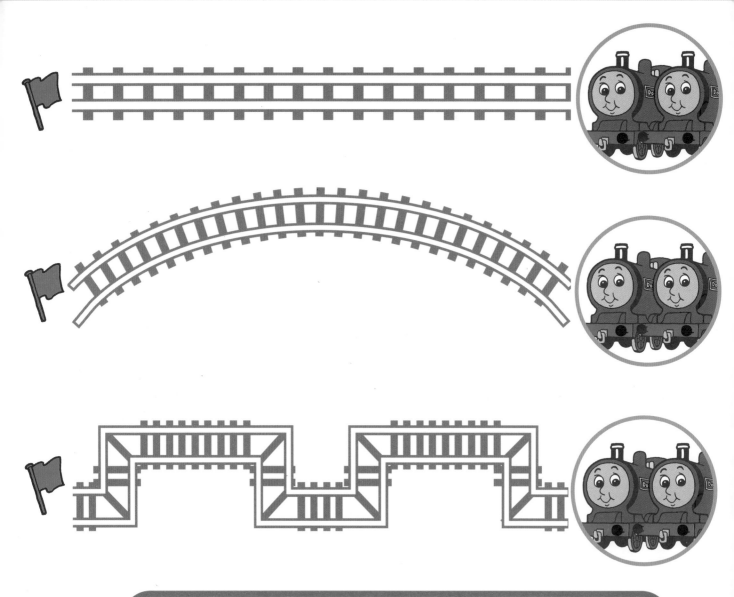

Follow the train tracks with your finger.
Start at the red flags.

Point to these things in the picture.

Spot the difference!

Point to 5 differences between these two pictures.

Thomas Reading

(age 4-6)

Develop your child's reading confidence with these six reading books, companion activity books and flash cards.

Thomas Maths

(age 4-6)

Introduce your child to early maths skills with these six maths story books, companion activity books and flash cards.